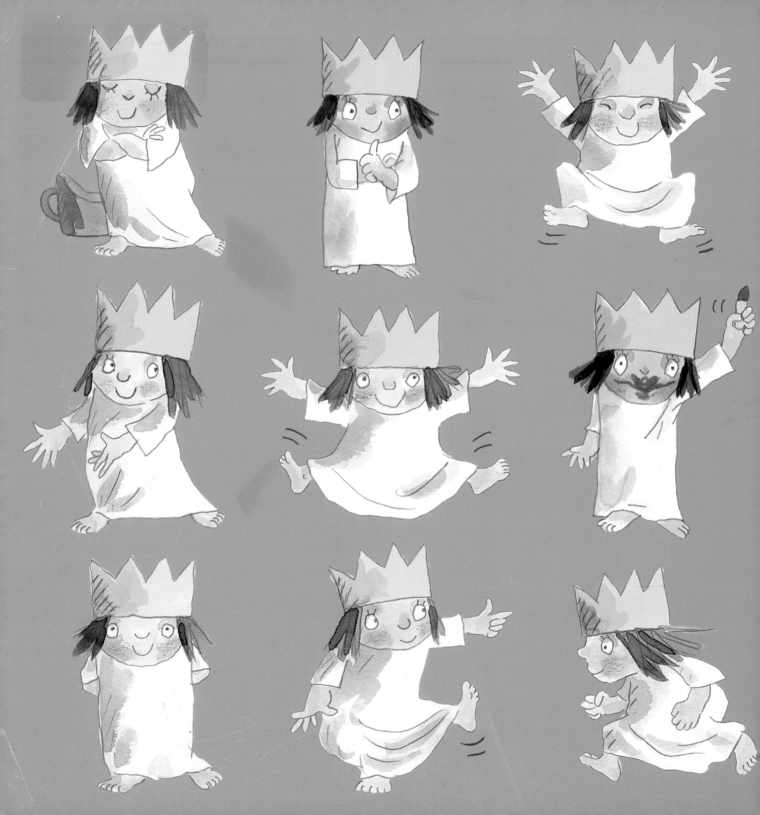

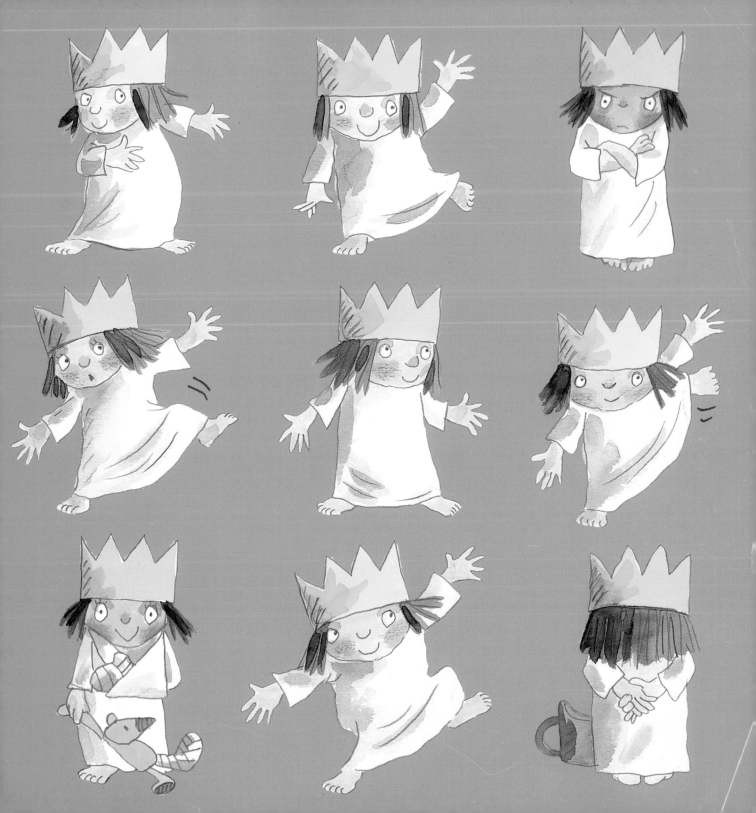

First published in hardback in Great Britain by Andersen Press Ltd in 2001,
based on an original version specially produced by Andersen Press Ltd for
*Domestos Hygiene Advisory Service* for promotional purposes only.
Text and illustrations copyright © Tony Ross 1998
This edition published in paperback by Collins Picture Books in 2003

5 7 9 10 8 6

ISBN-13: 978-0-00-715072-4
ISBN-10: 0-00-715072-5

Collins Picture Books is an imprint of the Children's Division, part of HarperCollins Publishers Ltd.

Text and illustrations copyright © Tony Ross 1998, 2001 and 2003

Visit our website at: www.harpercollinschildrensbooks.co.uk

Printed and bound in Hong Kong

# I Don't Want To Wash My Hands

## Tony Ross

HarperCollins *Children's Books*

"Wheeeeeeeeeee!"
The Little Princess LOVED getting dirty.

"Wash your hands before you eat that," said the Queen.
"Why?" said the Little Princess.

"Because you've been playing outside," said the Queen.

"Wash your hands," said the Cook.
"Why?" said the Little Princess.

"Because you've been playing with Scruff.
And dry them properly."

"Wash your hands," said the King.
"Why? I've washed them TWICE," said the Little Princess.

"And you must wash them again
because you've just been on your potty."

AAACHOOO

"Wash your hands," said the Maid.
"I don't want to wash my hands," said the Little Princess.

"I washed them after playing outside.
I washed them after playing with the dog.
I washed them after going on my potty.
I washed them after sneezing . . .

. . . WHY do I have to wash my hands?" said the Little Princess.
"Because of germs and nasties," said the Maid.
"What are germs and nasties?" said the Little Princess.

"They're HORRIBLE!" said the maid.

"They live in the dirties . . .

. . and on the animals . . .

. . . and in the sneezes.

Then they can get into your food,
and then into your tummy ...

... and then they make you ill."

"What do germs and nasties look like?" said the Little Princess.
"Worse than crocodiles," said the Maid.

"I've got no crocodiles on MY hands."

"Germs and nasties are smaller than crocodiles,"
said the Maid. "They are too small to see."

"I'd better wash my hands again," said the Little Princess.

"Do I have to wash my hands after washing my hands?"

"Don't be silly," said the maid. "Eat your cake."

"Have you washed YOUR hands?"

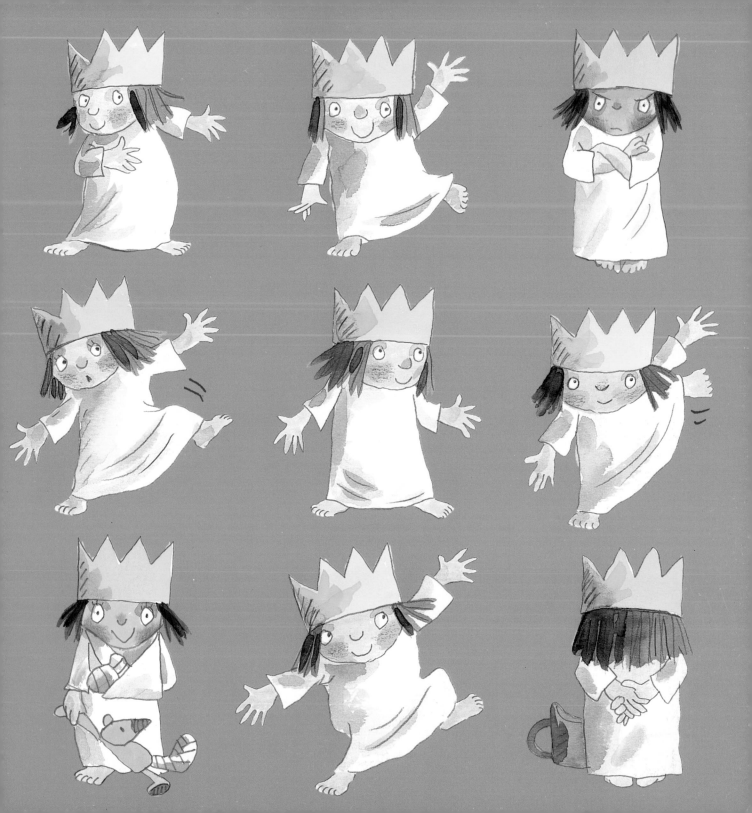

# Collect all the funny stories featuring the demanding Little Princess!

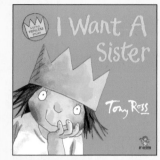

I Want My Potty

I Want To Be

I Want My Dinner

I Want A Sister

I Want My Dummy

I Don't Want To Wash My Hands

Tony Ross was born in London in 1938. His dream was to work with horses but instead he went to art college in Liverpool. Since then, Tony has worked as an art director at an advertising agency, a graphic designer, a cartoonist, a teacher and a film maker – as well as illustrating over 250 books! Tony, his wife Zoe and family live in Cheshire.